THE BRAVE LITTLE TOASTER

THE BRAVE LITTLE TOASTER

A BEDTIME STORY FOR SMALL APPLIANCES

by Thomas M. Disch

ILLUSTRATED BY KAREN SCHMIDT

DOUBLEDAY

NEW YORK   LONDON   TORONTO   SYDNEY   AUCKLAND

Published by DOUBLEDAY, a division of
Bantam Doubleday Dell Publishing Group, Inc.,
666 Fifth Avenue, New York, New York 10103.

DOUBLEDAY and the portrayal of an anchor with a dolphin
are trademarks of Doubleday, a division of
Bantam Doubleday Dell Publishing Group, Inc.

LIBRARY OF CONGRESS CATALOGING IN PUBLICATION DATA
Disch, Thomas M.
The brave little toaster.
Summary: Feeling abandoned by their beloved master,
a vacuum cleaner, tensor lamp, electric blanket, clock
radio, and toaster undertake a long and arduous journey
to find him in a faraway city.
[1. Fantasy]   I. Schmidt, Karen, ill.   II. Title.
PZ7.D6226Br   1986   [Fic]   85-12905
ISBN: 0-385-23050-8 TRADE EDITION

Lives there a man with soul so dead
He's never to his toaster said:
"You are my friend; I see in you
An object sturdy, staunch, and true;
A fellow mettlesome and trim;
A brightness that the years can't dim."?
Then let us praise the brave appliance
In which we place this just reliance.
And offer it with each fresh slice
Such words of friendship and advice
As "How are things with you tonight?"
Or "Not too dark but not too light."
                    Thomas M. Disch

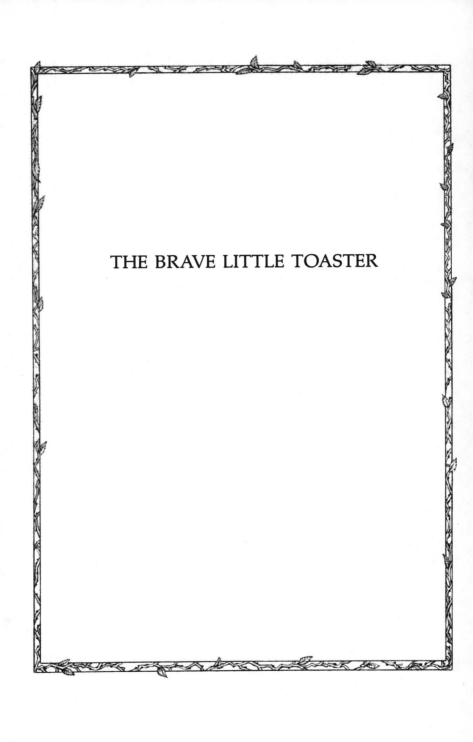

THE BRAVE LITTLE TOASTER

By the time the air conditioner had come to live in the summer cottage it was already wheezing and whining and going on about being old and useless and out-of-date. The other appliances had felt sorry and concerned, but when it finally did stop working altogether, they also felt a distinct relief. In all its time there it had never really been friendly—never really.

There were five appliances left in the cottage. The vacuum cleaner, being the oldest and a steady, dependable type besides (it was a Hoover), was their leader, insofar as they could be said to have one. Then there was an off-white plastic alarm clock/radio (AM only), a cheerful yellow electric blanket, and a Tensor lamp who had come from a savings bank and would sometimes get to speculating, late at night, whether that made him better than ordinary store-bought appliances or worse. Finally, there was the toaster, a bright little Sunbeam. It was the youngest member of the little clan, and the only one of them who had lived all its life there at the cottage, the other four having come with the master from the city years and years and years ago.

It was a pleasant cottage—quite cold in the winter, of course, but appliances don't mind that. It stood on the northernmost edge of an immense forest, miles from any neighbors and so far from the nearest highway that nothing was audible, day or night, but the peculiar hoots and rustlings of the forest and the reassuring sounds of the cottage itself—the creak of the timbers or the pattering of rain on windowpanes. They had grown set in their countrified ways and loved the little cottage dearly. Even if the chance had been offered them, which it wasn't, they wouldn't have wanted to be taken back to the city every year on Labor Day, the way that certain other appliances were, like the blender and the TV and the Water Pik. They *were* devoted to their master (that was just in their nature as appliances), but living so long in the woods had changed them in some nice, indefinable way that made the thought of any alternate life-style pretty nearly unthinkable.

The toaster was a special case. It had come straight to the cottage from a mail-order house, which tended to make it a little more curious about urban life than the other four. Often, left to itself, it would wonder what kind of toaster the master had in his city apartment, and it was privately of the opinion that whatever the brand of that other toaster it couldn't have made more perfect toast than the toaster made itself. Not too dark, not too light, but always the same uniform crunchy golden brown! However, it didn't come right out and say this in front of the others, since each of them was subject to periods of morbid misgivings as to its real utility. The old Hoover could maunder on for hours about the new breeds of vacuums with their low chassis, their long snaky hoses, and their disposable dust bags. The radio regretted that it couldn't receive FM. The blanket felt it needed a dry cleaning, and the lamp could never regard an ordinary 100-watt bulb without a twinge of envy.

But the toaster was quite satisfied with itself, thank you. Though it knew from magazines that there were toasters who could toast four slices at a time, it didn't think that the master, who lived alone and seemed to have few friends, would have wanted a toaster of such institutional proportions. With toast, it's quality that matters, not quantity: that was the toaster's credo.

Living in such a comfy cottage, surrounded by the strange and beautiful woods, you would have thought that the appliances would have had nothing to complain of, nothing to worry about. Alas, that was not the case. They were all quite wretched and fretful and in a quandary as to what to do—for the poor appliances had been abandoned.

"And the worst of it," said the radio, "is not knowing *why.*"

"The worst of it," the Tensor lamp agreed, "is being left in the dark this way. Without an explanation. Not knowing *what* may have become of the master."

11

"Two years," sighed the blanket, who had once been so bright and gay and was now so melancholy.

"It's more nearly two and a half," the radio pointed out. Being a clock as well as a radio, it had a keen sense of the passing time. "The master left on the twenty-fifth of September, 1973. Today is March 8, 1976. That's two years, five months, and thirteen days."

"Do you suppose," said the toaster, naming the secret dread none of them dared to speak aloud before, "that he knew, when he left, that he wouldn't be coming back? That he *knew* he was leaving us . . . and was afraid to say so? Is that possible?"

"No," declared the faithful old Hoover, "it is not! I can say quite confidently that our master would not have left a cottage full of serviceable appliances to . . . to rust!"

The blanket, lamp, and radio all hastened to agree that their master could never have dealt with them so uncaringly. Something had happened to him—an accident, an emergency.

"In that case," said the toaster, "we must just be patient and behave as though nothing unusual has happened. I'm sure that's what the master is counting on us to do."

And that is what they did. Every day, all through that spring and summer they kept to their appointed tasks. The radio/alarm would go off each morning at seven-thirty sharp, and while it played some easy-listening music, the toaster (lacking real bread) would pretend to make two crispy slices of toast. Or, if the day seemed special in some way, it would toast an imaginary English muffin. Muffins of whatever sort have to be sliced *very* carefully if they're to fit into a toaster's slots. Otherwise, when they're done, they may not pop out easily. Generally it's wiser to do them under a broiler. However, there *wasn't* a broiler in the cottage, nothing but an old-fashioned gas ring, and so the toaster did the best it could. In any case, muffins that are only imaginary aren't liable to get stuck.

Such was the morning agenda. In the afternoon, if it were a Tuesday or a Friday, the old Hoover would rumble about the cottage vacuuming up every scrap of lint and speck of dust. This involved little actual picking up, as it was rather a small cottage and was sealed very tight; so the dust and dirt had no way of getting inside, except on the days when the vacuum cleaner itself would trundle outdoors to empty a smidgen of dust at the edge of the forest.

At dusk the Tensor lamp would switch its switch to the ON position, and all five appliances would sit about in the kitchen area of the single downstairs room, talking or listening to the day's news or just staring out the windows into the gloomy solitude of the forest. Then, when it was time for the other appliances to turn themselves off, the electric blanket would crawl up the stairs to the little sleeping loft, where, since the nights were usually quite chilly, even in midsummer, it would radiate a gentle warmth. How the master would have appreciated the blanket on those cold nights! How safe and cozy he'd have felt beneath its soft yellow wool and electric coils! If only he'd been there.

At last, one sultry day toward the end of July, when the satisfactions of this dutiful and well-regulated life were beginning to wear thin, the little toaster spoke up again.

"We can't go on like this," it declared. "It isn't natural for appliances to live all by themselves. We need people to take care of, and we need people to take care of *us*. Soon, one by one, we'll all wear out, like the poor air conditioner. And no one will fix us, because no one will know what has happened."

"I daresay we're *all* of us sturdier than any air conditioner," said the blanket, trying to be brave. (Also, it is true, the blanket had never shown much fellow feeling for the air conditioner or any other appliances whose function was to make things cooler.)

"That's all very well for *you* to say," the Tensor lamp retorted. "You'll go on for years, I suppose, but what will become of me when my bulb burns out? What will become of the radio when its tubes start to go?"

The radio made a dismal, staticky groan.

"The toaster is right," the old Hoover said. "Something must be done. Something definitely must be done. Do any of you have a suggestion?"

"If we could telephone the master," said the toaster, thinking aloud, "the radio could simply ask him outright. *He'd* know what we should do. But the telephone has been disconnected for nearly three years."

14

"Two years, ten months, and three days, to be exact," said the radio/alarm.

"Then there's nothing else for us to do but to find the master ourselves."

The other four appliances looked at the toaster in mute amazement.

"It isn't unheard of," the toaster insisted. "Don't you remember—only last week there was a story that the radio was telling us, about a dear little fox terrier who'd been accidentally left behind, like us, at a summer cottage. What was his name?"

"Grover," said the radio. "We heard it on the 'Early Morning Roundup.'"

"Right. And Grover found his way to his master, hundreds of miles away in a city somewhere in Canada."

"Winnipeg, as I recall," said the radio.

"Right. And to get there he had to cross swamps and mountains and face all sorts of dangers, but he finally did find his way. So, if one silly dog can do all that, think what five sensible appliances, working together, should be able to accomplish."

"Dogs have legs," the blanket objected.

"Oh, don't be a wet blanket," the toaster replied in a bantering way.

It should have known better. The blanket, who didn't have much of a sense of humor and whose feelings were therefore easily hurt, began to whimper and complain that it was time for it to go to bed. Nothing would serve, finally, but that the toaster should make a formal apology, which it did.

"Besides," said the blanket, mollified, "dogs have noses. That's how they find their way."

"As to that," said the old Hoover, "I'd like to see the nose that functions better than mine." And to demonstrate its capabilities it turned itself on and gave a deep, rumbling snuffle up and down the rug.

"Splendid!" declared the toaster. "The vacuum shall be our nose—and our legs as well."

The Hoover turned itself off and said, "I beg your pardon?"

"Oh, I meant to say our *wheels.* Wheels, as I'm sure everyone knows by now, are really more efficient than legs."

"What about the rest of us," the blanket demanded, "who don't have wheels *or* legs? What shall *we* do? I can't *crawl* all the way to wherever it is, and if I tried to, I'd soon be shredded to rags."

The blanket was certainly in a fretful state, but the toaster was a born diplomat, answering every objection in a tone of sweet, unswervable logic.

"You're entirely right, and the radio and I would be in an even sorrier state if we tried to travel such a distance on our own. But that isn't necessary. Because we'll *borrow* some wheels. . . ."

The Tensor lamp lighted up. "And build a kind of carriage!"

"And *ride* all the way there," said the radio, "in comfort and luxury." It sounded, at such moments, exactly like the announcer in an advertisement.

"Well, I'm not sure," said the blanket. "I *might* be able to do that."

"The question is," said the toaster, turning to the Hoover, "will *you* be able to?"

Deep in its motor the vacuum cleaner rumbled a rumble of quiet confidence.

IT was not as easy a matter as the toaster had supposed to find a serviceable set of wheels. Those he'd had in mind at first belonged to the lawn mower out in the lean-to shed, but the task of disconnecting them from the mower's heavy blades was beyond the appliances' limited know-how. So, unless the Hoover were willing to cut a swatch of lawn everywhere it went, which it wasn't, the lawn mower's sturdy rubber wheels had to be put out of mind.

The blanket, who was now full of the spirit of adventure, suggested that the bed in the sleeping loft might be used, since it had four caster-type wheels. However, the weight and unwieldiness of the bed were such as to rule out that notion as well. Even on a level road the Hoover would not have had the strength to draw such a load—much less across raw wilderness!

And that seemed to be that. There were no other wheels to be found anywhere about the cottage, unless one counted a tiny knife sharpener that worked by being rolled along the countertop. The toaster racked its brains trying to turn the knife sharpener to account, but what kind of carriage can you build with a single wheel that is one and a half inches in diameter?

Then, one Friday, as the Hoover was doing its chores, the idea the toaster had been waiting for finally arrived. The Hoover, as usual, had been grumbling about the old metal office chair that stood in front of the master's desk. No amount of nudging and bumping would ever dislodge its tubular legs from where they bore down on the rug. As the vacuum became more and more fussed, the toaster realized that the chair would have moved very easily . . . *if it had still possessed its original wheels!*

It took the five appliances the better part of an afternoon to jack up the bed in the sleeping loft and remove the casters. But it was no trouble at all to put them on the chair. They slipped right into the tubular legs as though they'd been made for it. Interchangeable parts *are* such a blessing.

And there it was, their carriage, ready to roll. There was quite enough room on the padded seat for all four riders, and being so high it gave them a good view besides. They spent the rest of the day delightedly driving back and forth between the cottage's overgrown flower beds and down the gravel drive to the mailbox. There, however, they had to stop, for that was as far as the Hoover could get, using every extension cord in the cottage.

"If only," said the radio with a longing sigh, "I still had my old batteries. . . ."

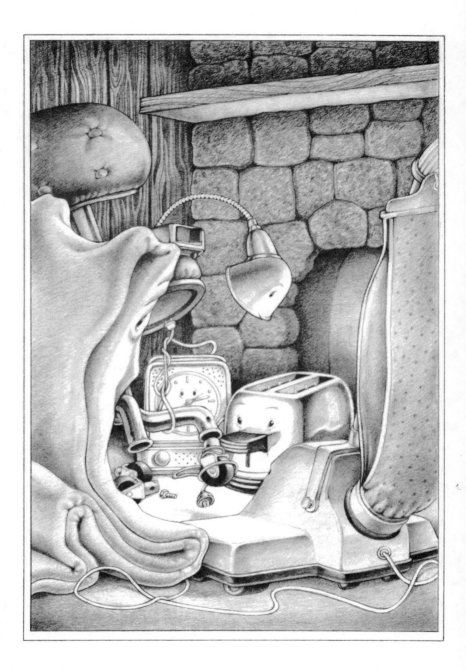

"Batteries?" inquired the toaster. "I didn't know you had batteries."

"It was before you joined us," said the radio sadly. "When I was new. After my first batteries corroded, the master didn't see fit to replace them. What need had I for batteries when I could always use the house current?"

"I don't see what possible relevance your little volt-and-a-half batteries could have to *my* problem," observed the Hoover testily.

The radio looked hurt. Usually the Hoover would never have made such an unkind and slighting remark, but the weeks of worry were having their effect on all of them.

"It's *our* problem," the toaster pointed out in a tone of mild reproof, "and the radio is right, you know. If we *could* find a large enough battery, we could strap it under the seat of the chair and set off this very afternoon."

"If!" sniffed the Hoover scornfully. "If! If!"

"And I know where there may be a battery as big as we need!" the Tensor lamp piped. "Have you ever looked inside that lean-to behind the cottage?"

"Into the toolshed!" said the blanket with a shudder of horror. "Certainly not! It's dark and musty and filled with spiders."

"Well, I was in it just yesterday, poking about, and there was *something* behind the broken rake and some old paint cans—a big, black, boxy thing. Of course it was nothing like *your* pretty red cylinders." The Tensor lamp tipped its hood toward the radio. "But now that I think of it, it may have been a *kind* of battery."

The appliances all trooped out to the lean-to, and there in the darkest corner, just as the lamp had supposed, was the spare battery that had come from the master's old Volkswagen. The battery had been brand-new at the time that he'd decided to trade in the VW on a yellow Saab, and so he'd replaced it with a less valuable battery, keeping this one in the lean-to and then—wasn't it just his way?—forgetting all about it.

Between them, the old Hoover and the toaster knew enough about the basic principles of electricity to be able, very quickly, to wire the battery so that it would serve their needs instead of an automobile's. But before any of the small appliances who may be listening to this tale should begin to think that they might do the same thing, let them be warned: ELECTRICITY IS VERY DANGEROUS. *Never* play with old batteries! *Never* put your plug in a strange socket! And if you are in any doubt about the voltage of the current where you are living, *ask a major appliance.*

And so they set off to find their master in the faraway city where he lived. Soon the dear little summer cottage was lost from sight behind the leaves and branches of the forest trees. Deeper and deeper they journeyed into the woods. Only the dimmest dapplings of sunlight penetrated through the dense tangle overhead to guide them on their way. The path wound around and twisted about with bewildering complex-

ity. The road map they had brought with them proved quite useless.

It would have been ever so much easier, of course, to have followed the highway directly into the city, since that is where highways always go. Unfortunately that option was not open to them. Five such sturdy and functional appliances would certainly not have been able to escape the notice of human beings traveling along the same thoroughfare, and it is a rule, which all appliances must obey, that whenever human beings are observing them they must remain perfectly still. On a busy highway they would therefore have been immobilized most of the time. Besides, there was an even stronger reason for staying off the highway— the danger of pirates. But that's a possibility so frightening and awful that we should all simply refuse to think any more about it. Anyhow who ever heard of pirates in the middle of the woods?

The path twisted and turned and rose and fell, and the poor old Hoover became very tired indeed. Even with the power from the battery it was no easy task making its way over such a rugged terrain, especially with the added burden of the office chair and its four riders. But except for its rumbling a little more loudly than usual the old vacuum cleaner did its job without a complaint. What a lesson for us all!

As for the rest of them, they were in the highest spirits. The lamp craned its long neck every which way, exclaiming over the views, and even the blanket soon forgot its fears and joined in the general spirit of holiday adventuring. The toaster's coils were in a continual tingle of excitement. It was all so strange and interesting and full of new information!

"Isn't it wonderful!" exclaimed the radio. "Listen! Do you hear them? Birds!" It did an imitation of the song it had just heard—not one that would have fooled any of the actual birds there in the forest, for in truth it sounded more like a clarinet than a bird. Even so, a thrush, a wood pigeon, and several chickadees did come fluttering down from their roosts and perches high above to cock their heads and listen. But only a moment. After a twitter or two of polite approval they returned to the trees. Birds are like that. They'll pay attention to you for a minute or two and then go right back to being birds.

The radio pretended not to feel slighted, but it soon left off doing imitations and recited, instead, some of its favorite ads, the beautiful songs about Coca-Cola and Esso and a long comic jingle about Barneys' Hi-Styles for Guys and Gals. There's nothing that so instantly civilizes a forest as the sound of a familiar advertisement, and soon they were all feeling a lot more confident and cheerful.

As the day wore on, the Hoover was obliged to stop for a rest more and more frequently—ostensibly to empty its dust bag. "Can you believe," it grieved, shaking a last moldering leaf from the bag, "how filthy this forest is?"

"On the contrary," the blanket declared. "It's thoroughly agreeable. The air's so fresh, and just feel the breeze! I feel renewed, as if I'd just come out of my original box. Oh, why, why, why don't they ever take electric blankets on picnics? It isn't fair!"

"Enjoy it while it lasts, kiddo," said the radio ominously. "According to the latest Weather and Traffic Roundup, we're in for rain."

"Won't the trees work like a roof?" asked the lamp. "They keep the sunlight out well enough."

None of them knew the answer to the lamp's question, but as it happens, trees do not work like a roof. They all got more or less wet, and the poor blanket was drenched through and through. Fortunately the storm did not last long and the sun came out immediately afterward. The wet appliances trudged on along the muddy path, which led them, after a little while, to a clearing in the wood. There in a glade full of sunshine and flowers the blanket was able to spread itself out on the grass and begin to get dry.

The afternoon was wearing on, and the toaster had begun to feel, as all of us do at times, a definite need for solitude. Much as it liked its fellow appliances, it wasn't used to spending the entire day socializing. It longed to be off by itself a moment to be private and think its own thoughts. So, without saying anything to the others, it made its way to the farthest corner of the meadow and began to toast an imaginary muffin. That was always the best way to unwind when things got to be too much for it.

The imaginary muffin had scarcely begun to warm before the toaster's reveries were interrupted by the gentlest of interrogatories.

"Charming flower, tell me, do,
What genera and species you
Belong to. I, as may be seen
At once, am just a daisy, green
Of leaf and white of petal. You
Are neither green nor white nor
*   blue*
Nor any color I have known.
In what Eden have you grown?
Sprang you from earth or sky
*   above?*
In either case, accept my love."

"Why, thank you," the toaster replied, addressing the daisy that was pressing its petaled face close to the toaster's gleaming chrome. It's kind of you to ask, but in fact I'm not a flower at all. I'm an electric toaster."

"Flower, forbear! You can't
*   deceive*
The being that adores you. Weave
Your thick black root with mine.
O beautiful! O half-divine!"

These fervent declarations so embarrassed the toaster that for a moment it was at a loss for words. It had never heard flowers speaking in their own language and didn't realize how they would say any absurd thing that would help them to a rhyme. Flowers, as botanists well know, can speak only in verse. Daisies, being among the simpler flowers, characteristically employ a rough sort of octosyllabic doggerel, but more evolved species, especially those in the tropics,

26

can produce sestinas, rondeaux, and villanelles of the highest order.

The daisy was not, however, simply snared in its own rhyme scheme. It had genuinely fallen in love with the toaster—or, rather, with its own reflection in the toaster's side. Here was a flower (the daisy reflected) strangely like itself and yet utterly unlike itself too. Such a paradox has often been the basis for the most impassioned love. The daisy writhed on its stem and fluttered its white petals as though in the grip of cyclone winds.

The toaster, thoroughly alarmed by such immoderate behavior, said that it really was time to be getting back to its friends on the other side of the meadow.

> *"Oh, stay, beloved blossom,*
>   *stay!*
> *They say our lives are but a day:*
> *If that be true, how shall I bear*
> *To spend that brief day anywhere*
> *Except with you? You are my*
>   *light,*
> *My soil, my air. Stay but one*
>   *night*
> *Beside me here—I ask no more.*
> *Stay, lovely bloom—let me adore*
> *Those polished petals bright as the*
>   *dew*
> *When dawn attempts to rival you,*
> *That single perfect coiling root—*
> *Imperishable! Absolute!*
> *O beautiful! O half-divine!*
> *Weave your thick black root with*
>   *mine."*

"Now really," said the toaster in a tone of gentle reprimand, "there's no cause to be carrying on like this. We scarcely know each other and, what's more, you seem to be under a misapprehension as to my nature. Can't you see that what you call my root is an electric cord? As to petals, I can't think *what* you may mean, for I simply don't have any. Now—I really must go and join my friends, for we are journeying to our master's apartment far, far away, and we shall never get there if we don't get a move on."

"Alas the day and woe is me!
I tremble in such misery
As never flower knew before.
If you must go, let me implore
One parting boon, one final gift:
Be merciful as you are swift
And pluck me from my native
* ground—*
Pluck me and take me where
* you're bound.*
I cannot live without you here:
Then let your bosom be my bier."

Feeling truly shocked by the daisy's suggestion and seeing that the creature was deaf to reason, the toaster hastened to the other side of the meadow and began to urge its friends to set out at once on their journey. The blanket protested that it was still somewhat damp, the Hoover that it was still tired, and the lamp proposed that they spend the night there in the meadow.

And that is what they did. As soon as it grew dark the blanket folded itself into a kind of tent, and the others all crawled inside. The lamp turned itself on, and the radio played some easy-listening music—but very quietly, so as not to disturb other denizens of the forest who might already be asleep. Soon they were asleep themselves. Travel does take it out of you.

T HE alarm clock had set itself, as usual, for seven-thirty, but the appliances were awake well before that hour. The vacuum cleaner and the lamp both complained, on rising, of a certain stiffness in their joints. However, as soon as they were on their way, the stiffness seemed to melt away.

In the morning light the forest appeared lovelier than ever. Cobwebs glistening with dew were strung like miniature power lines from bough to bough. Pretty mushrooms sprouted from fallen logs, looking for all the world like a string of frosted light bulbs. Leaves rustled. Birds chirped.

The radio was certain that it saw a real fox and wanted to go off after it. "Just to be sure, you know, that it *is* a fox."

The blanket grew quite upset at this suggestion. It had already snagged itself once or twice on low-hanging branches. What ever would become of it, it wanted to know, if it were to venture from the path and into the dense tangle of the forest itself.

"But think," the radio insisted, "—a fox! We'll never have such a chance again."

"I'd like to see it," said the lamp.

The toaster, too, was terribly curious, but it could appreciate the blanket's point of view, and so it urged them to continue along the path. "Because, don't you see, we must reach the master as soon as we possibly can."

This was so inarguably true that the radio and lamp readily assented, and they continued on their way. The sun rose in the sky until it had risen all it could, and the path stretched on and on. In the midafternoon there was another shower, after which they once again made camp. Not, this time, in a meadow, for the woods were now quite dense, and the only open places were those under the larger trees. So instead of sunning itself on the grass (for there was neither grass nor sunlight to be found), the blanket hung itself, with the Hoover's help, from the lowest limb of an immense and ancient oak. In minutes it had flapped itself dry.

At twilight, just as the lamp was thinking of turning itself on, there was a stir among the leaves on the branch to the right of the branch from which the blanket was contentedly hanging.

"Hello!" said a squirrel, emerging from the clustered leaves. "I *thought* we had visitors."

"Hello," replied all the appliances together.

"Well, well, well!" The squirrel licked his whiskers. "What do you say then, eh?"

"About what?" asked the toaster, who was not be-

ing unfriendly, but who could be a little literal-minded at times, especially when it was tired.

The squirrel looked discountenanced. "Allow me to introduce myself. I'm Harold." Having pronounced his name, his good humor seemed completely restored. "And this fair creature—"

Another squirrel dropped from a higher branch and lighted beside Harold.

"—is my wife, Marjorie."

"Now you must tell us your names," said Marjorie, "since we've just told you ours."

"We don't have names, I'm afraid," said the toaster. "You see, we're appliances."

"If you don't have names," Harold demanded, "how do you know which of you are men and which are women?"

"We aren't either. We're appliances." The toaster turned to the Hoover for confirmation.

"Whatever *that* may mean," said Marjorie brusquely. "It can't alter a universal law. Everyone is either a man or a woman. Mice are. Birds are. Even, I'm given to understand, insects." She held her paw up to her lips and tittered. "Do you like to eat insects?"

"No," said the toaster. "Not at all." It would have been more trouble than it was worth to explain to the squirrels that appliances didn't eat anything.

"Neither do I, *really*," said Marjorie. "But I love nuts. Do you have any with you? Possibly in that old sack?"

"No," said the Hoover stiffly. "There is nothing in

that old sack, as you call it, but dirt. About five pounds of dirt, I'd estimate."

"And what is the use, pray, of saving dirt?" asked Harold. When no answer seemed forthcoming, he said, "I know what we'd all enjoy doing. We can tell jokes. You start."

"I don't think I know any jokes," said the Hoover.

"Oh, I do," said the radio. "You're not Polish, are you?"

The squirrels shook their heads.

"Good. Tell me—why does it take three Poles to screw in a light bulb?"

Marjorie giggled expectantly. "I don't know—why?"

"One to hold the light bulb, and the other two to turn the ladder around."

The squirrels looked at each other with bewilderment.

"Explain it," said Harold. "Which are the men and which are the women?"

"It doesn't matter. They're just very stupid. That's the whole idea of Polish jokes, that Poles are supposed to be so stupid that no matter what they try and do they misfunction. Of course, it's not fair to Poles, who are probably as bright as anyone else, but they are funny jokes. I know hundreds more."

"Well, if that was a fair sample, I can't say I'm very keen to hear the rest," said Marjorie. "Harold, you tell him—"

"It," the radio corrected. "We're all its."

"Tell *them,*" Marjorie continued, "the one about the

three squirrels out in the snow." She turned to the lamp confidingly. "This will lay you out. Believe me."

As Harold told the joke about the three squirrels in the snow, the appliances exchanged glances of guarded disapproval. It wasn't just that they disapproved of dirty jokes (especially the old Hoover); in addition, they didn't find such jokes amusing. Gender and the complications it gives rise to simply aren't relevant to the lives appliances lead.

Harold finished his joke, and Marjorie laughed loyally, but none of the appliances cracked a smile.

"Well," said Harold, miffed, "I hope you enjoy your stay under *our* oak."

With which, and a flick of their big furry tails, the two squirrels scampered up the trunk and out of sight.

In the small hours of the night the toaster woke from a terrible nightmare in which it had been about to fall into a bathtub full of water to discover itself in a plight almost as terrible. Thunder was thundering, and lightning was streaking the sky, and rain was pelting it mercilessly. At first the toaster couldn't remember where it was or why it was there, and when it did remember, it realized with dismay that the electric blanket, which ought to have been spread out and sheltering the other four appliances, had disappeared! And the rest of them? They were still here, thank heaven, though in a state of fearful apprehension, each one of them.

"Oh dear," groaned the Hoover, "I should have

known, I should have *known!* We never, never should have left our home."

The lamp in an extremity of speechless agitation was twisting its head rapidly from side to side, casting its little beam of light across the gnarled roots of the oak, while the radio's alarm had gone off and would not stop ringing. Finally the toaster went over to the radio and turned the alarm off itself.

"Oh, thank you," said the radio, its voice blurry with static. "Thank you so much."

"Where is the blanket?" the toaster demanded apprehensively.

"Blown away!" said the radio. "Blown off to the far end of the forest, where we shall never be able to find it!"

"Oh, I should have *known!"* groaned the Hoover. "I should have *known!"*

"It's not your fault," the toaster assured the vacuum, but it only groaned the louder.

Seeing that it could not be of any help to the vacuum, the toaster went over to the lamp and tried to calm it down. Once its beam was steady, the toaster suggested that it be directed into the branches above them, on the chance that the blanket, when it was blown away, might have been snagged on one of them. The lamp did so, but it was a very faint light and a very tall oak and a very dark night, and the blanket, if it were up there, was not to be seen.

All of a sudden there was a flash of lightning. The radio's alarm went off again, and the lamp shrieked and folded itself up as small as could be. Of course it's silly to be afraid of lightning, since it's only another form of electricity. But such a large form—and so uncontrolled! If you were a person, instead of an appliance, and you encountered a berserk giant many times larger than yourself, you'd have some idea how the average electric appliance feels about lightning.

In the brief moment that the lightning was lighting everything up, the toaster, who had been peering up into the oak, was able to make out a shape—all twisted about—that *might* have been the blanket. The toaster waited until there was another lightning flash; and, yes, definitely, it *was* the yellow blanket, which had indeed become snagged on one of the highest branches of the tree.

Once they all knew that the blanket was nearby, even though they still had no idea how they'd be able to get it down, the storm ceased to seem quite so scary. The rain made them quite miserable, as rain will do, but their worst anxieties were over. Even the occasional bolt of lightning was now something to be wished for rather than dreaded, since by its brightness they could glimpse their companion high above them, clutching to the limb of the oak and flailing in the ceaseless winds. How could they feel afraid, or even sorry for themselves, when they considered the terrors the poor blanket must be experiencing?

By morning the storm had abated. The radio, at top volume, called up to the blanket, but the blanket made no response. For one horrible moment the toaster thought its friend might have stopped working altogether. But the radio kept on calling to the blanket, and after a time it made a feeble reply, waving one wet bedraggled corner at its friends.

"YOU CAN COME DOWN NOW," the radio shouted. "THE STORM IS OVER."

"I *can't,*" said the blanket with a whimper. "I'm stuck. I *can't* get down."

"You must try," the toaster urged.

"What's that?" said the blanket.

"THE TOASTER SAYS YOU MUST TRY!"

"But I told you—I'm *stuck.* And there's a great rip right through the center of me. And another by my hem. And I hurt." The blanket began to wring itself convulsively, and a steady patter of droplets fell from its rain-soaked wool into the puddles below.

"What the deuce is all this racket about?" Harold demanded imperiously, stepping forth from his nest high in the trunk of the oak. "Do you have any idea what *time* it is? Squirrels are trying to sleep."

The radio apologized to Harold and then explained the cause of the commotion. Like most squirrels, Harold was essentially kind-hearted, and when he saw what had happened to the blanket, he immediately offered his assistance. First he went into his nest and woke his wife. Then together the two squirrels began to help the blanket to loosen itself from where it had been snared. It was a long and—to judge by the blanket's cries—painful process, but at last it was done, and with the squirrels' help the liberated blanket made its way, slowly and carefully, down the trunk of the tree.

The appliances gathered around their friend, com-

miserating over its many injuries and rejoicing at its rescue.

"How shall we ever be able to repay you?" said the toaster warmly, turning to Harold and Marjorie. "You've saved our friend from a fate too terrible to imagine. We're *so* grateful."

"Well," said Marjorie cagily, "I can't remember whether or not you said you had any nuts with you. But if you do. . . ."

"Believe me," said the Hoover, "if we did, you would have them all. But you can see for yourselves that my bag contains nothing but dust and dirt." Whereupon it opened its dust bag and a thick brown sludge of rain-sodden topsoil oozed forth.

"Though we don't have nuts," said the toaster to the disconsolate squirrels, "perhaps there is something *I* could do for you. That is, if you like *roasted* nuts."

"Indeed, yes," said Harold. "Any kind will do."

"Then if you can provide me with some nuts, I shall roast them. As many as you like."

Harold narrowed his eyes suspiciously. "You mean you want us to give *you* the nuts *we've* been storing up all this summer?"

"If you'd like me to roast them," answered the toaster brightly.

"Oh, darling, do," Majorie urged. "I don't know what he means to do, but *he* seems to. And we might like it."

"I think it's a trick," said Harold.

"Just two or three of the ones that are left from last year. Please?"

"Oh, very well."

Harold scampered up the tree trunk to his nest and returned with four acorns stuffed in the pouches of his cheeks. At the toaster's bidding Harold and Majorie cracked them open, and then Harold placed them carefully on the thin strips of metal that went up and down inside the toaster's slots. As these strips were meant to accommodate large slices of bread, it had to be very careful lest the tiny round acorns should roll off as it lowered them into itself. When this was done it turned on its coils and commenced toasting them. When the acorns were starting to turn a crispy brown, the toaster lifted them up gently as far as it could, turned off its coils, and (when it judged the squirrels would not burn their paws by reaching in) bade them take out the roasted nuts and taste them.

"Delicious!" Majorie declared.

"Exquisite!" Harold agreed.

As soon as the squirrels had eaten the first four acorns, they returned to their nest for more, and when those were gone still more, and then again some more after that. Marjorie, especially, was insatiable. She urged the toaster to remain in the forest as their guest. It could stay in their own nest, where it would always be dry and cozy, and she would introduce it to all their friends.

"I'd love to be able to accept," said the toaster, from a sense not only of politeness but of deep obligation as well, "but it really isn't possible. Once I've roasted your nuts for you—would you like some more?—we *must* be on our way to the city where our master lives."

While the toaster roasted some more acorns, the radio explained to the squirrels the important reason for their journey. It also demonstrated its own capacities as a utensil and persuaded the other appliances to do the same. The poor Hoover was scarcely able to function from having been clogged with mud, and the squirrels, in any case, could not see the point of sweeping up dirt from one place and putting it somewhere else. Nor did the lamp's beams or the radio's music excite their admiration. However, they were both very taken with the electric blanket, which, damp as it was, had plugged itself into the battery strapped under the office chair and was glowing warmly. Marjorie renewed her invitation to the toaster and extended it to the blanket as well. "Until," she explained, "you're quite well again."

"That's very kind," said the blanket, "and of course I'm *so* grateful for all you've done. But we must be on our way. Truly."

Marjorie sighed resignedly. "At least," she said, "keep your tail tucked into that black thing that makes the furry part of you so delightfully hot. Until you have to leave. The warmth is so pleasant. Isn't it, my dear?"

"Oh, yes," said Harold, who was busy shelling acorns. "Most agreeable."

The Hoover ventured a mild protest, for it feared that with both the toaster and the blanket working so hard the battery would be worn down needlessly. But really what else could they do but comply with the squirrels' request? Besides, quite apart from their debt of gratitude, it felt so good to be useful again! The toaster would have gone on gladly roasting acorns all morning and all afternoon, and the squirrels seemed of much the same disposition.

"It's strange," said Harold complacently, while he stroked the toaster's side (now sadly streaked with raindrop patterns like the outside of a window), "it's more than strange that you should maintain you have no sex, when it's very clear to me that you're male." He studied his own face in the mottled chromium. "You have a man's whiskers and a man's front teeth."

"Nonsense, darling," said his wife, who was lying on the other side of the toaster. "Now that I look carefully, I can see her whiskers are most definitely a woman's whiskers and teeth as well."

"I won't argue, my love, about anything so patently obvious as whether or not a man is a man, for it's evident that he is!"

It suddenly dawned on the toaster how the squirrels —and the daisy the day before—had come by their confusions. They were seeing *themselves* in its sides! Living in the wild as they did, where there are no bathroom mirrors, they were unacquainted with the principle of reflectivity. It considered trying to explain their error to them, but what would be the use? They would only go away with hurt feelings. You can't always expect people, or squirrels, to be rational. Appliances, yes—appliances have to be rational, because they're built that way.

To Harold the toaster explained, under seal of strictest secrecy, that it was indeed, just as he had supposed, a man; and to Marjorie it confided, under a similar pact of trust, that it was a woman. It hoped they were both true to their promises. If not, their argument would be fated to continue for a long, long while.

With its coils turned to HIGH, the blanket was soon quite dry, and so, after a final round of roast acorns, the appliances said goodbye to Harold and Marjorie and continued on their way.

A_ND what a long and weary way it was! The forest stretched on seemingly forever with the most montonous predictability, each tree just like the next —trunk, branches, leaves; trunk, branches, leaves. Of course a tree would have taken a different view of the matter. We all tend to see the way *others* are alike and how *we* differ, and it's probably just as well we do, since that prevents a great deal of confusion. But perhaps we should remind ourselves from time to time that ours is a very partial view, and that the world is full of a great deal more variety than we ever manage to take in. At this stage of their journey, however, the appliances had lost sight of this important truth, and they were very bored and impatient, in addition simply to being worn to a frazzle. Rust spots had begun to develop alarmingly on the unchromed bottom of the toaster and inside it as well. The stiffness that the vacuum and lamp complained of each morning on rising no longer vanished with a bit of exercise but persisted through the day. As for the blanket, it was almost in tatters, poor thing. Alone of the appliances, the radio seemed not to have suffered damage from the demands of the trip.

The toaster began to worry that when they did at last arrive at the master's apartment they would be in such raggle-taggle condition that he would have no further use for them. They'd be put on the scrap heap, and all their efforts to reach him would have been in vain! What a dreadful reward for so much loyalty and devotion! But it is a rare human being who will be swayed by considerations of the heart in his dealings with appliances, and the master, as the toaster well knew, was not notable for his tender conscience. Its own predecessor at the cottage had still been quite serviceable when it had been sent to the dump, its only faults having been that its chrome had been worn away in patches and that its sense of timing was sometimes erratic. In its youth the toaster had thought these sufficient grounds for the older appliance's replacement, but now . . .

Now it was better not to think about such matters. Better simply to pursue one's duty wherever it led, along the path through the forest.

Until, at the bank of a wide river, that path finally came to an end.

They were all, at first sight of that broad impassable expanse of water, utterly cast down and despairing, none more so than the Hoover, which became almost incoherent in its distress. "No!" it roared aloud. "I refuse! Never! Oh! Stop, turn me off, empty my bag, leave me alone, go away!" It began to choke and sputter, and then ran over its own cord and started chewing on it. Only the toaster had enough presence of mind to wrest the cord from the vacuum's powerful suction grip. Then, to calm it down, it led the Hoover back and forth across the grassy bank of the river in regular, carpet-sweeping swathes.

At last these habitual motions brought the Hoover around to a more reasonable frame of mind, and it was able to account for its extraordinary alarm. It was not only the sight of this new obstacle that had distressed it so, but, as well, its certainty that the battery was now too run-down for them to be able to return to the cottage by its power. They could not go forward and they could not turn back. They were marooned! Marooned in the middle of the forest, and soon it would be fall and they would have no shelter from the inclemencies of the autumn weather, and then it would be winter and they'd be buried in the snow. Their metal parts would corrode. The Hoover's rubber belt would crack. They would be powerless to resist the forces that would slowly but surely debilitate and destroy them, and in only a few months—or even weeks—they would all be unable to work.

No wonder the Hoover, foreseeing this inevitable

progression of events, had been beside itself. What *were* they to do? the toaster asked itself.

There was no answer immediately forthcoming.

Toward evening the radio announced that it was receiving interference from a source quite nearby. "A power drill, by the feel of it. Just on the other side of the river."

Where there was a power drill there were bound to be power lines as well! New hope poured into the appliances like a sudden surge of current.

"Let's look at the map again," said the lamp. "Maybe we can figure out exactly where we are."

Following the lamp's suggestion, they unfolded the road map and looked very carefully at all the dots and squiggles between the spot (marked with a Magic Marker) along the highway where the cottage was situated and the little patch of pink representing the city they were bound for. At last, only a quarter inch from the pink patch of the city, they found the wavery blue line that had to be the river they'd come to, since there were no other blue lines anywhere between the cottage and the city, and this river was much too big for the mapmakers to have forgotten all about it.

"We're almost there!" the radio trumpeted. "We'll make it! Everything will be all right! Hurrah!"

"Hurrah!" the other appliances agreed, except for the Hoover, who wasn't so easily convinced that all would now be well. But when the lamp pointed out four distinct places where the river was traversed by highways, even the Hoover had to admit that there was cause to cheer up, though it still wouldn't go so far as to say "Hurrah."

"We only have to follow the river," said the toaster, who did like to give instructions, even when it was obvious what had to be done, "either to the left or the right, and eventually it must lead us to one of those bridges. Then, when it's very late and there's no traffic, we can make a dash for it!"

So once again they set off with courage renewed and determination strengthened. It was not so light a task as the toaster had made it sound, for there was no longer a clear path to follow. Sometimes the bank of the river lay flat as a carpet, but elsewhere the ground got quite bumpy or—what was worse—quaggy and soft. Once, avoiding a rock, the Hoover took a sharp turn; and the office chair, getting a leg mired in an unremarked patch of mud, was overturned, and the four appliances riding on it tumbled off the plastic seat into a thorough slough. They emerged smirched and spattered, and were obliged to become dirtier still in the process of retrieving the caster wheel that had come off the chair and was lost in the mud.

The blanket, naturally, was exempted from this task, and while the four others delved for the lost wheel, it betook itself down the water's edge and attempted to wash away the signs of its spill. Lacking any cloth or sponge, the blanket only succeeded, sad to say, in spreading the stains over a larger area. So preoccupied was the blanket with its hopeless task that it almost failed to notice—

"A boat!" the blanket cried out. "All of you, come here! I've found a boat!"

Even the toaster, with no experience at all in nautical matters, could see that the boat the blanket had discovered was not of the first quality. Its wood had the weather-beaten look of the clapboard at the back of the summer cottage that the master had always been meaning to replace, or at least repaint, and its bottom must be leaky for it was filled with one big puddle of green mush. Nevertheless, it must have been basically serviceable, since a Chris-Craft outboard motor was mounted on the blunt back end, and who would put an expensive motor on a boat that couldn't at least stay afloat?

"How providential," said the Hoover.

"You don't intend for us to *use* this boat, do you?" asked the toaster.

"Of course we shall," replied the vacuum. "Who knows how far it may be to a bridge? This will take us across the river directly. You're not afraid to ride in it, are you?"

"Afraid? Certainly not!"

"Well, then?"

"It doesn't *belong* to us. If we were to take it, we'd be no better than . . . than pirates!"

Pirates, as even the newest of my listeners will have been informed, are people who take things that belong to other people. They are the bane of an appliance's existence, since once an appliance has been spirited away by a pirate, it has no choice but to serve its bidding just as though it were that appliance's legitimate master. A bitter disgrace, such servitude—and one that few appliances can hope to escape once it has fallen to their lot. Truly, there is no fate, even obsolescence, so terrible as falling into the hands of pirates.

"Pirates!" exclaimed the Hoover. "Us? What nonsense? Who ever heard of an appliance that was a pirate?"

"But if we took the boat—" the toaster insisted.

"We wouldn't *keep* it," said the Hoover brusquely. "We'd just borrow it a little while to cross the river and leave it on the other side. Its owner would get it back soon enough."

"How long we'd have it for doesn't matter. It's the *principle* of the thing. Taking what isn't yours is piracy."

"Oh, as for principles," said the radio lightly, "there's a well-known saying: *'From* each according to his abilities, *to* each according to his needs.' Which means, as far as I can see, that someone who makes use of his abilities should get to use a boat when he or it needs to cross a river and the boat is just sitting there waiting." With which, and a little chuckle besides, the radio hopped onto the foremost seat of the rowboat.

Following the radio's example, the Hoover heaved the office chair into the back of the boat and then got in itself. The boat settled deep in the water.

Avoiding the toaster's accusing look, the blanket took a seat beside the radio.

The lamp seemed to hesitate, but only for a moment. Then it too entered the boat.

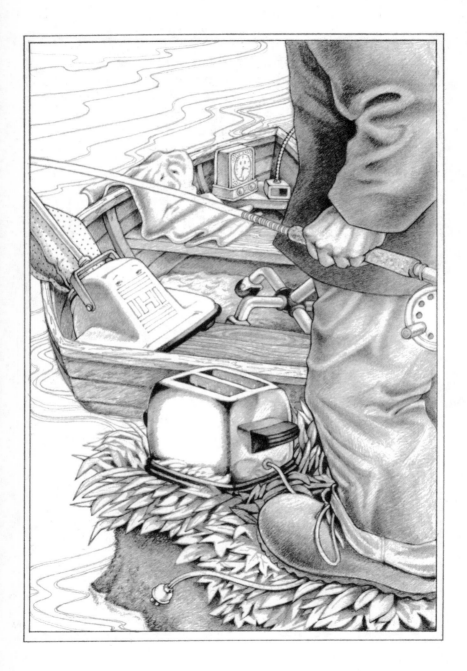

"Well?" said the Hoover gruffly. "We're waiting."

Reluctantly the toaster prepared to board the boat. But then, inexplicably, *something made it stop.* What's happening? it wondered—though it could not say the words aloud, for the same force preventing it from moving prevented its speech as well.

The four appliances in the boat had been similarly incapacitated. What had happened, of course, was that the owner of the boat had returned and *seen* the appliances. "Why, what's this?" he exclaimed, stepping from behind a willow tree with a fishing rod in one hand and a string of sunfish in the other. "It seems we've had some visitors!"

He said much more than this, but in a manner so rough and ill-mannered that it is better not to repeat his words verbatim. The sum of it was this—that he believed the owner of the appliances had been about to steal his boat, and so he intended, by way of retaliation, to steal the appliances!

He took the toaster from where it sat spellbound on the grassy riverbank and set it in the rowboat beside the blanket, lamp, and radio. Then, unfastening the battery from the office chair, he threw the latter end-over-end high up into the air. It came down—Splash!—in the middle of the river and sank down to the muddy bottom, nevermore to be seen.

Then the pirate—for there could no longer be any doubt that such he was—started the Chris Craft motor and set off upstream with his five helpless captives.

After mooring his boat alongside a ramshackle dock on the other side of the river, the pirate loaded the outboard motor and the appliances onto the wooden bed of a very dusty pickup truck—except for the radio, which he took with him into the front seat. As it drove off, the truck jolted and jounced and bolted and bounced so violently the toaster feared the ride would cost it every coil in its body. (For though toasters look quite sturdy, they are actually among the more delicate appliances and need to be handled accordingly.) But the blanket, realizing the danger the toaster was in, managed to slip underneath its old friend and cushion it from the worst shocks of the journey.

As they rode they could hear the radio in the front seat humming the poignant theme song from *Doctor Zhivago*.

"Listen!" the Hoover hissed. "Of all possible songs to be singing, it has chosen one of the master's favorites. Already it has forgotten him!"

"Ah," said the toaster, "what choice does it have, poor thing? Once one of us had been turned on, would we have behaved any otherwise? Would you? Would I?"

The old vacuum groaned, and the radio went on playing its sad, sad song.

WHAT graveyards are for people—horrible, creepy places that any reasonable individual tries to stay away from—the city dump is for appliances and machines of every description. Imagine, therefore, what the appliances must have felt when they realized (the pirate had parked his pickup in front of a high, ripply iron gate and was opening the padlock with a key from the ring that swung from his belt) that they had been brought to the city dump! Imagine their horror as he drove the truck inside and they assimilated the terrible fact that he lived here! There, with smoke curling from a tin chimney, was his wretched shack—and all about it the most melancholy and fearsome sights the toaster had ever witnessed. Dismembered chassis of once-proud automobiles were heaped one atop the other to form veritable mountains of rusted iron. The asphalt-covered ground was everywhere strewn with twisted beams and blistered sheet metal, with broken and worn-out machine parts of all shapes and sizes—with all the terrible emblems, in short, of its own inevitable obsolescence. An appalling scene to behold—yet one that exercised a strange fascination over the toaster's mind. As often as it had heard of the city dump, it had somehow never really believed in its existence. And now it was here, and nothing, not even the pirate's stony gaze, could prevent its shudder of fear and wonder.

The pirate got out of the truck and took the radio, along with his fishing rod and his day's catch, into the hovel where he lived. The appliances, left to themselves in the back of the truck, listened to the radio sing song after song with apparently indefatigable good cheer. Among them was the toaster's own favorite melody, "I Whistle a Happy Tune." The toaster was certain this couldn't be a coincidence. The radio was trying to tell its friends that if they were brave and patient and cheerful, matters would work out for the best. Anyhow, whether that was the radio's intention or just a program it had been tuned to, it was what the toaster firmly believed.

After he'd had his dinner the pirate came out of his shack to examine the other appliances. He fingered the Hoover's mud-stained dust bag and the frayed part of its cord where it had been chewing on itself. He lifted the blanket and shook his head in mute deprecation. He looked inside the lamp's little hood and saw— which the lamp itself had not realized till now—that its tiny bulb was shattered. (It must have happened when the lamp had fallen off the office chair, just before they'd found the boat.)

Finally the pirate picked up the toaster—and made a scornful grimace. "Junk!" he said, depositing the toaster on a nearby scrap pile.

"Junk!" he repeated, dealing with the lamp in a similar fashion.

"Junk!" He hurled the poor blanket over the projecting, broken axle of a '57 Ford.

"Junk!" He set the Hoover down on the asphalt with a shattering *thunk.*

"All of it, just junk." Having delivered this dismaying verdict, the pirate returned to his shack, where the radio had gone on singing in the liveliest manner all the while.

"Thank goodness," said the toaster aloud, as soon as he was gone.

"Thank goodness?" the Hoover echoed in stricken tones. "How can you say 'Thank goodness' when you've just been called junk and thrown on a heap of scrap?"

"Because if he'd decided to take us into his shack and use us, we'd have become his, like the radio. This way we've got a chance to escape."

The blanket, where it hung, limply, from the broken axle, began to whimper and whine. "No, no, it's true. That's all I am now—junk! Look at me—look at these tears, these snags, these stains. Junk! This is where I belong."

The lamp's grief was quieter but no less bitter. "Oh, my bulb," it murmured, "oh, my poor, poor bulb!"

The Hoover groaned.

"Pull yourselves together, all of you!" said the toaster, in what it hoped was a tone of stern command. "There's nothing wrong with any of us that a bit of fixing up won't put right. You—" It addressed the blanket. "—are still fundamentally sound. Your coils haven't been hurt. After some sewing up and a visit to the dry cleaner you'll be as good as new."

It turned to the lamp. "And what nonsense—to fuss over a broken bulb! You've broken your bulb before and probably will many times again. What do you think replaceable parts are *for?*"

Finally the toaster directed its attention to the vacuum cleaner. "And you? You, who must be our leader! Who ought to inspire us with your own greater strength! For *you* to sit there groaning and helpless! And just because some old pirate who lives in a dump makes an unflattering remark. Why, he probably doesn't even know how to *use* a vacuum cleaner— that's the sort of person *he* is!"

"Do you think so?" said the Hoover.

"Of course I do, and so would you if you'd be rational. Now, for goodness' sake, let's all sit down together and figure out how we're going to rescue the radio and escape from here."

By midnight it was amazing how much they'd managed to accomplish. The Hoover had recharged the run-down battery from the battery in the pirate's own truck. Meanwhile the lamp, in looking about for another doorway or gate than the one they'd come in by (there wasn't any), had discovered a vehicle even better suited to their needs than the office chair the pirate had thrown in the river. This was a large vinyl perambulator, which is another word for pram, which is also known, in the appliances' part of the world, as a baby buggy. By whatever name, it was in good working order—except for two minor faults. One fault was a squeak in the left front wheel, and the other was the

56

way its folding visor was twisted out of shape so as to give the whole buggy an air of lurching sideways when it was moving straight ahead. The squeak was fixed with a few drops of 3-in-One Oil, but the visor resisted their most determined efforts to bend it back into true. But that didn't matter, after all. What mattered was that it *worked*.

To think how many of the things consigned to this dump were still, like the buggy (or themselves, for that matter) essentially serviceable! There were hair dryers and four-speed bicycles, water heaters and wind-up toys that would all have gone on working for years and years with just the slightest maintenance. Instead, they'd be sent to city dump! You could hear their hopeless sighs and crazed murmurings rising from every dark mound around, a ghastly medley that seemed to swell louder every moment as more and more of the forlorn, abandoned objects became conscious of the energetic new appliances in their midst.

"You will never, never, never get away," whispered a mad old cassette player in a cracked voice. "No, never! You will stay here like all the rest of us and rust and crack and turn to dust. And never get away."

"We will, though," said the toaster. "Just you wait and see."

But how? That was the problem the toaster had to solve without further delay.

Now the surest way to solve any problem is to think about it, and that's just what the toaster did. It thought with the kind of total, all-out effort you have to give to get a bolt off that's rusted onto a screw. At

first the bolt won't budge, not the least bit, and the wrench may slip loose, and you begin to doubt that any amount of trying is going to accomplish your purpose. But you keep at it, and use a dab of solvent if there's any on hand, and eventually it starts to give. You're not even sure but you think so. And then, what do you know, it's off! You've done it! That's the way the toaster thought, and at last, because it thought so hard, it thought of a way they could escape from the pirate and rescue the radio at the same time.

"Now here's my plan," said the toaster to the other appliances, which had gathered around it in the darkest corner of the dump. "We'll *frighten* him, and that will make him run away, and when he's gone we'll go into his shack—"

"Oh, no, I *couldn't* do that," said the blanket with a shiver of dread.

"We'll go into his shack," the toaster insisted calmly, "and get the radio and put it inside the baby buggy and get in ourselves, all except the Hoover, of course, which will hightail it out of this place just as fast as it can."

"But won't the gate be locked?" the lamp wanted to know. "It is now."

"No, because the pirate will have to unlock it to get out himself, and he'll be too frightened to remember to lock it behind him."

"It's a very good plan," said the Hoover, "but what I don't understand is—*how* are we going to frighten him?"

"Well, what are people afraid of the most?"

"Getting run over by a steamroller?" the Hoover guessed.

"No. Scarier than that."

"Moths?" suggested the blanket.

"No."

"The dark," declared the lamp with conviction.

"That's close," said the toaster. "They're afraid of ghosts."

"What are ghosts?" demanded the Hoover.

"Ghosts are people who are dead, only they're also sort of alive."

"Don't be silly," said the lamp. "Either they *are* dead or they aren't."

"Yes," the blanket agreed. "It's as simple as ON and OFF. If you're ON, you can't be OFF, and vice versa."

"*I* know that, and *you* know that, but people don't seem to. People say they know that ghosts don't exist but they're afraid of them anyhow."

"No one can be afraid of something that doesn't exist," the Hoover huffed.

"Don't ask me how they do it," said the toaster. "It's what they call a paradox. The point is this—people are afraid of ghosts. And so *we're* going to pretend to be one."

"How?" asked the Hoover skeptically.

"Let me show you. Stoop down. Lower. Wrap your cord around my cord. Now—lift me up. . . ."

After an hour's practice of pretending to be a ghost, they decided they were ready. Carefully, so that the other appliances wouldn't fall off, the old Hoover trundled toward the window of the shack. The toaster, where it was balanced atop the handle of the vacuum, was just able to see inside. There on a table between a stack of unwashed dishes and the pirate's ring of keys was the poor captive radio, and there, in dirty striped pajamas, getting ready to go to bed, was the pirate.

"Ready?" the toaster whispered.

The blanket, which was draped over the vacuum in a roughly ghostlike shape with a kind of hood at the top through which the toaster was able to peer out, adjusted its folds one last time. "Ready," the blanket replied.

"Ready?" the toaster asked again.

For just a moment the lamp, where it was hidden halfway down the handle of the Hoover, turned itself on and then, quickly, off. The bulb it had taken from the socket in the ceiling of the pickup truck had only half the wattage it was used to, and so its beam of light was noticeably dimmer—just enough to make the blanket give off the faintest yellowish glow.

"Then let's start haunting," said the toaster.

That was the signal the Hoover had been waiting for.

"Whoo!" groaned the Hoover in its deepest, most quivery voice. "Whoo!"

The pirate looked up with alarm. "Who's there?" he demanded.

"Whoo—oo!" the Hoover continued.

"Whoever you are, you'd better go away."

"Whoo—oo—oo!"

Cautiously the pirate approached the window from which the groaning seemed to issue.

Upon receiving a secret electric signal from the toaster, the vacuum crept quietly alongside the shack to where they would be out of sight from the window.

"Whoo . . ." breathed the Hoover in the barest of whispers. "Whoo . . . Whoo—oo . . ."

"Who's out there?" the pirate demanded, pressing his nose against the pane of glass and peering into the outer darkness. "You'd better answer me. Do you hear?"

In answer the Hoover made a strangling, gurgling, gaspy sound that sounded frightening even if you knew it was only the Hoover doing it. By now the pirate, who didn't have any idea what this mysterious groaning might be, had got into a considerable state of nerves. When you live all alone in the city dump you don't expect to hear strange noises just outside your window in the middle of the night. And if you were also a bit superstitious, as pirates tend to be . . .

"All right then—if you won't say who you are, I'm going to come out there and find out!" He lingered yet a while before the window, but at last, when no reply was forthcoming, the pirate pulled on his pants and then got into his boots. "I'm warning you!" he called out, though not in a tone that could be called threatening.

Still there was no reply. He took up his key ring from where it lay on the table beside the radio. He went to the door.

He opened it.

"Now!" said the toaster, signaling secretly to the blanket along its electric cord.

"I can't," said the blanket, all atremble. "I'm too afraid."

"You *must!*"

"I mustn't: it's against the rules."

"We discussed all that before, and you *promised.* Now hurry—before he gets here!"

With a shudder of trepidation the blanket did as it was bidden. There was a tear in its side where it had been pierced by a branch on the night it was blown up into the tree. The lamp was hiding just behind this rent. As the pirate appeared around the corner of the shack, the blanket twitched the torn fabric aside.

The pirate stopped short in his tracks when he saw the shrouded figure before him.

"Whoo—oo!" groaned the Hoover one last time.

At this cue the lamp turned itself on. Its beam slanted up through the hole in the blanket right into the pirate's face.

When the lamp lit up, the pirate stared at the figure before him with the utmost horror. What he saw that was so frightening was the same thing the daisy had seen, the same thing Harold and Marjorie had seen, as well—he saw his own features reflected in the toaster's mottled chrome. And as he had been a very wicked person from his earliest youth, his face had taken on that special kind of ugliness that only very evil people's faces acquire. Seeing such a face grimacing at him from this strange hooded figure, what was the pirate to suppose but that he had come upon the most dan-

gerous kind of ghost, the kind that understands exactly who we are and knows all the wrong things we've done and intends to punish us for them. From such ghosts even grown-up pirates will flee in terror. Which is exactly what the pirate did.

As soon as he was gone, the appliances rushed into the pirate's shack and rescued the joyful radio. Then before the pirate could return they scrambled into the baby buggy, and the old Hoover drove off with them as fast as its wheels would revolve.

As luck would have it, they didn't have much farther to go: where the master lived on Newton Avenue was only a mile or so from city dump. They reached his apartment building early in the morning before a single milk truck had appeared on the street.

"You see," said the toaster cheerfully, "in the end everything really does work out for the best."

Alas, the toaster had spoken too soon. Their tribulations were not yet at an end, and not everything would work out for the best, as they were shortly to discover.

The Hoover, which had an instinctive knack for such things, buzzed the street door open and summoned the automatic elevator. When the elevator door slid open, it wheeled the buggy in and pressed the button for the fourteenth floor.

"It's *changed* so," said the Tensor lamp, as the Hoover pushed the buggy out of the elevator and down the corridor. "The wallpaper used to be green squiggles and white blobs, and now it's crisscross lines."

"It's we who've changed," said the blanket miserably.

"Hush," said the Hoover sternly. "Remember the rules!" It pressed the doorbell beside the door to the master's apartment.

All the appliances kept perfectly still.

No one came to the door.

"Maybe he's asleep," said the alarm clock/radio.

"Maybe he's not home," said the Hoover. "I'll see." It rang the doorbell again, but in a different way so that only the appliances in the apartment would be able to hear it ring.

In only a moment a Singer sewing machine answered the door. "Yes?" said the sewing machine in a tone of polite curiosity. "Can I help you?"

"Oh, excuse me, I seem to have made a mistake." The Hoover looked at the number on the door, then at the name on the brass panel over the bell. It was the right number, the right name. But . . . a sewing machine?

"Is that . . . ?" said a familiar voice within the apartment. "Why, it is! It's the old Hoover! How *are* you? Come in! Come in!"

The Hoover wheeled the buggy into the apartment and over the deep-piled carpet toward the friendly old TV.

The blanket peeked out shyly over the side of the buggy.

"And who's that with you? Come out—don't be shy. My goodness, what a treat this is."

The blanket crawled out of the buggy, taking care to keep the worst effects of the journey folded up out of sight. It was followed by the radio, the lamp and, last of all, the toaster.

The TV, which knew all five of them from the time it had spent with the master at the summer cottage, introduced them to the many appliances from all over the apartment which had begun to gather in the living room. Some, like the Water Pik, the blender, and the TV itself, were old friends. Some, like the stereo and the clock on the mantel, were known to the four appliances that had lived in the apartment at one time themselves but not to the toaster. But a great many were complete strangers to them all. There were huge impractical ginger-jar lamps squatting on low tables and, out of the bedroom, dim little lamps with frilly shades and other lamps screwed into the dining nook wall that were pretending to be candle flames. Out of the kitchen had trooped a whole tribe of unfamiliar gadgets: a Crock-Pot, a can opener, a waffle iron, a meat grinder, a carving knife, and, somewhat abashedly, the master's new toaster.

"How do you do," said the new toaster in a barely audible voice when the TV introduced it.

"How do *you* do?" the toaster replied warmly.

Neither could think of anything else to say. Fortunately there were more introductions to be effected.

The Hoover had to go through a similar ordeal when it met the apartment's vacuum cleaner, which was (just as the Hoover had feared) one of the new lightweight models that looks like a big hamburger bun on wheels. They were polite to each other, but it was obvious that the new vacuum looked on the Hoover as outmoded.

The blanket had an even worse shock in store. The last two appliances to appear in the living room were a vaporizer and a long tangled string of Christmas tree lights, both of which had been hibernating in a closet. The blanket looked about anxiously. "Well," it said, making a determined effort to seem accepting and friendly, "I think there must still be one more of you we haven't yet met."

"No," said the TV. "We're all here."

"But is there no other . . . blanket?"

The TV avoided the blanket's earnest gaze. "No. The master doesn't use an electric blanket anymore. Just a plain wool one."

"But he always . . . he always . . ." The blanket could say no more. Its resolution deserted it and it fell in a heap on the carpet.

A gasp went up from the apartment's assembled appliances, which until now had had no idea of the extent of the blanket's injuries.

"Doesn't *use* an electric blanket!" the toaster repeated indignantly. "Whyever not?"

The screen of the TV flickered and then, evasively, started showing a gardening show.

"It isn't the master's choice, really," said the Singer

sewing machine in its funny clipped accent. "I daresay *he* would be delighted to see his old blanket again."

The blanket looked up questioningly.

"It's the mistress," the sewing machine went on. "She says she becomes too hot under an electric blanket."

"The mistress?" the five appliances repeated.

"Didn't you know?"

"No," said the toaster. "No, we haven't heard anything from the master since he left the cottage three years ago."

"Two years, eleven months, and twenty-two days, to be precise," said the alarm clock/radio.

"That's why we determined to find our way here. We feared . . . I don't know what exactly. But we thought that . . . that our master would need us."

"Oh," said the sewing machine. It turned to watch the gardening show on the TV.

As unobtrusively as it might, the new toaster crept back into the kitchen and resumed it post of duty on the formica countertop.

"Two years, eleven months, and twenty-two days is a long time to be left alone," the radio asserted at rather a loud volume. "Naturally we became concerned. The poor air conditioner stopped working altogether."

"And all the while," said the lamp, "never a word of explanation!" It glared reproachfully at the TV, which continued to discuss the problem of blister beetles.

"Can't *any* of you tell us why?" the toaster demanded earnestly. "Why did he never return to the cottage? There must be a *reason.*"

"I can tell you," said the vaporizer, inching forward. "You see, the mistress is subject to hay fever. I can help her a bit with her asthma, but when the hay fever starts in on her, there's nothing anyone can do, and she is really very miserable then."

"I still don't understand," said the toaster.

The sewing machine spelled it out. "Rather than go to the country, where there is bound to be ragweed and pollen and such, they spend their summers at the seaside."

"And our cottage—our lovely cottage in the woods —what is to become of it?"

"I believe the master means to sell it."

"And . . . and us?" the toaster asked.

"I understand there is to be an auction," said the sewing machine.

The Hoover, which had comported itself with great dignity throughout the visit, could bear no more. With a loud groan it grasped the handle of the buggy as though to steady itself. "Come," it gasped. "All of you, come. We are not wanted here. We'll return to . . . to . . ."

Where would they return? Where could they? They had become appliances without a household!

"To the dump!" shrieked the blanket hysterically. "Isn't that where *junk* belongs? That's all we are now —junk!" It twisted its cord into an agonized knot. "Isn't that what the pirate said we were? Junk! Junk! Junk! All of us, and me most of all."

"Control yourself," said the toaster sternly, though its own coils felt as though they were about to snap. "We're *not* junk. We're sturdy, useful appliances."

"Look at me!" cried the blanket, displaying the full extent of its worst tear. "And these mud stains—look!"

"Your tears can be sewn up," said the toaster calmly. It turned to the sewing machine. "Can't they?"

The sewing machine nodded in mute agreement. "And the stains can be cleaned."

"And then what?" the Hoover demanded dourly. "Let us suppose the blanket is repaired and cleaned, and that I've mended my cord and got my dust bag into working shape, and that you've polished yourself. Suppose all that—what then? Where shall we go?"

"I don't know. Somewhere. I'll have to think."

"Pardon me," said the TV, turning off the gardening show. "But didn't I hear you say something about a . . . pirate?"

"Yes," said the sewing machine nervously. "What pirate did you mean? There's not a pirate in this building, I hope?"

"Never fear—we don't have to worry anymore about him. He captured us but we escaped from him. Would you like to know how?"

"Goodness, yes," said the TV. "I love a good story."

So all the appliances gathered in a circle about the toaster, which began to tell the story of their adventures from the moment they had decided to leave the cottage till the moment they arrived at the door of the apartment. It was a very long story, as you know, and while the toaster told it, the sewing machine set to work sewing up all the rips and tears in the blanket.

THE next afternoon when the blanket came back from Jiffy Dry Cleaners on the other side of Newton Avenue, the apartment's appliances put on a splendid party for their five visitors. The Christmas tree lights strung themselves up between the two ginger-jar lamps and winked and bubbled in the merriest way, while the TV and the stereo sang duets from all the most famous musical comedies. The toaster was polished to a fare-thee-well, and the Hoover was likewise in fine fettle once again. But most wonderful of all— the blanket looked almost as good as new. Its yellow was possibly not as bright as it had been, but it was a lovely yellow, for all that. The exact same yellow, according to the TV, of custard and primroses and the nicest bathroom tissues.

At five o'clock the radio's alarm went off, and everyone became very still, except for the blanket, which went on whirling gaily about the living room for some time before it realized the music had stopped.

"What is it?" asked the blanket. "Why are you all so quiet?"

"Hush," said the radio. "It's time for 'The Swap Shop.'"

"What is 'The Swap Shop?' " asked the blanket.

"It's the program on listener-supported radio station KHOP," said the toaster excitedly, "that is going to find a new home for us! I told you not to worry, didn't I? I told you I'd think of something!"

"Be quiet," said the lamp. "It's starting."

The radio turned up its volume so that all the appliances in the living room could hear. "Good afternoon," it said, in a deep, announcer-type voice, "and welcome to 'The Swap Shop.' Today's program opens with a very strange offering from Newton Avenue. It seems that someone there wants to swap—now listen to this list!—a Hoover vacuum cleaner, an AM alarm clock/radio, a yellow electric blanket, a Tensor lamp, and a Sunbeam toaster. All this in exchange for . . . well, it says on the card here: 'You name it.' What's most important, I'm informed, is that you should have a real and genuine *need* for all five of these fine appliances, since their present owner wants them to be able to stay together. For sentimental reasons! Now I've heard everything! Anyhow, if you think you *need* those five appliances, the number to call is KL5-9120. That number again, KL5-9120. Our next offer is not quite so unusual. Seems there's a party on Center Street who is offering, absolutely for free, five lovable black-and-white—"

The radio tuned out KHOP. "Didn't he make us sound super!" it exclaimed, forgetting in its excitement to stop speaking in the announcer's voice.

"Come over here by the telephone," the Hoover

urged the radio. "You'll have to talk to them. I'm just too nervous."

All five appliances gathered about the telephone and waited for it to ring.

There are two schools of thought about whether or not appliances ought to be allowed the free use of telephones. Some insist that it is flatly against the rules and should never be done in any circumstances, while others maintain that it's all right, since it is only another appliance one is talking to, in this case a telephone. Whether or not it's against the rules, it is certainly a fact that a good many appliances (lonely radios especially) do use the phone system regularly, usually to contact other appliances. This explains the great number of so-called "wrong numbers" that people get at odd times. Computerized exchanges could never make so many mistakes, though they end up taking the blame.

For the last three years, of course, this issue had not mattered very much to the appliances, since the phone in the cottage had been disconnected. Ordinarily, the Hoover would probably have opposed the notion of any of them using the phone, as it did tend to adopt the conservative attitude. But first there had been the absolute necessity of calling Jiffy Dry Cleaners and having them pick up the blanket, and that had established a clear precedent for their phoning in to KHOP and offering themselves on "The Swap Shop." And now here they were all gathered around the telephone, waiting to talk with their next master!

The phone rang.

"Now whatever you do," warned the Hoover, "don't say yes to the first person who happens to call. Find out something about him first. We don't want to go just anywhere, you know."

"Right," said the radio.

"And remember," said the toaster, "to be nice."

The radio nodded. It picked up the telephone receiver. "Hello?" it said.

"Is this the person with the five appliances?"

"It is! Oh my goodness yes indeed, it is!"

And so the five appliances went to live with their new mistress, for as it happened it was a woman who'd phoned them first and not a man. She was an elderly, impoverished ballerina who lived all alone in a small room at the back of her ballet studio on Center Street in the oldest part of the city. What the ballerina had swapped for the appliances were her five lovable black-and-white kittens. The appliances' former master never could figure out how, upon returning with his wife from their summer vacation by the sea, there had come to be five kittens in their apartment. It was rather an awkward situation, for his wife was allergic to cat fur. But they were such darlings—it would never have done to put them out on the street. In the end they decided to keep them, and his wife simply took more antihistamines.

And the appliances?

Oh, they were *very* happy. At first the Hoover had been doubtful about entering service with a woman (for it had never worked for a woman before, and it was somewhat set in its ways), but as soon as it realized what a fastidious and immaculate housekeeper its mistress was, it forgot all its reservations and became her greatest champion.

It felt so good to be *useful* again! The radio would play beautiful classical music for the ballerina to dance to; and when she became tired and wanted to sit down and read, the lamp would light her book; and then when it grew late and she'd finished her book, the blanket would give off a steady, gentle warmth that kept her cozy all through the long, cold night.

And when it was morning and she awoke, what wonderful slices of toast the toaster would toast for her—so brown and crisp and perfect and always just the same!

And so the five appliances lived and worked, happy and fulfilled, serving their dear mistress and enjoying each other's companionship, to the end of their days.

Tom Disch lives most of the time in New York City, where he has toast for breakfast every day toasted by the little, two-slice toaster who has been working with the author for over fifteen years, and whose friendly and faithful service, sense of humor, and good toast was a constant inspiration to Mr. Disch, when he wrote THE BRAVE LITTLE TOASTER, his first book for children.

He is the author of a number of books of fiction (among them, the award-winning science fiction novel *On Wings of Song*) and poetry (including a book entitled *Abcdefg Hijklmn Poqrst Uvwxyz*).

Karen Schmidt was born in Albuquerque, New Mexico, and grew up in Taiwan, Virginia, and Apple Valley, California. She attended Santa Barbara Art Institute, the Oregon School of Art, and then moved to New York City, where she attended the School of Visual Arts and the Art Students League. She now makes her home in New York City and frequently visits Apple Valley.

She has been illustrating children's books since 1983 and has eight books in print.